Chili Chinchilla

Written by Donna MacLeod
Illustrated by Maddy Moore

Briley & Baxter Publications | Plymouth, Massachusetts

ISBN: 978-1-954819-98-6

Book Design: Stacy Padula

To my son Kyle who created the very first image of Chili.

Deep in the Andes Valley lives a chinchilla named Chili,
Unlike any you've seen before.
She wears a coat of argentine blue,
Too beautiful to ignore.

Although she is beautiful, sometimes she is sad,
For she is never invited to play.
The animals think she is far too different,
And laugh at her day after day.

Then one day as he passes,
Hector Hedgehog winks an eye.
"Don't you listen to them," he says.
"Don't you let them make you cry."

"Keep wearing that radiant smile,
And hold your head up high.
I don't understand these creatures,"
Hector mutters with a sigh.

So Chili went about her day,
Gathering some food to eat.
She stored it in a tree hollow,
And came back later for her treat.

But when she returned, her food was gone,
Not a nut could be found.
She looked high, and she looked low,
She dug deeply in the ground.

She felt a tear well up in one eye,
And in the other, too.
She gulped and swallowed and quietly said,
"Now what am I to do?"

Then she heard a faint rustling,
And looked back through the trees.
Hector Hedgehog had come back,
With a basket of nuts and leaves.

"I thought you might need me,"
He said now rather sure.
"You seem to be a little sadder,
Than you were before."

"I don't know why they're mean to me,"
Chili dropped her head and sighed.
"I think I am a good chinchilla,"
She sniffled and she cried.

"Of course you're good," said Hector,
"And you have done no wrong,
You've been so kind and patient,
While trying to belong."

"If you treat your foe with kindness,
You will beat them at their game.
Show them who you really are,
And how we're all the same."

So the next day, Chili set out,
Gathering food for the day.
She spied a group of young chinchillas,
And asked them to come and play.

They smirked and tossed their heads up high,
"We cannot play with you.
You really ought to know by now,
You simply are too blue!"

"But in my basket, I'd like to share,
Some tasty nuts you see.
Wouldn't you like some, I'm sure you would,
Here, come sit next to me."

The chinchillas moved very slowly,
Not knowing what to think.
Then they sat beneath a grand old tree,
To share some food and drink.

After they ate, they frolicked around,
Then became too tired to run,
They paused for a moment and bowed their heads.
They had never had so much fun!

"You're really very nice," they said,
"Not unlike us in the least.
And because we have been so mean and cruel,
We would like to return your feast."

There before Chili was her basket,
With everything in place.
Suddenly she was feeling very lucky,
And had a smile upon her face!

Her eyes shone bright and she said,
"This is very kind of you.
I'm sure that we can be such good friends!"
And soon their friendship grew.

Deep in the Andes Valley, lives a chinchilla named Chili,
Who became a friend to all.
Every creature in the valley,
Every creature, big and small.

About the Author

Donna MacLeod's passion for writing has been a lifelong pursuit, fueled by the inspiration received from her college journalism professor. Even though she was a business major, her love for creative writing evolved, and after penning a book on personal loss in 2009, her desire for creative writing continued to grow. This led her to write this book intended to educate young children on the differences between people and the importance of acceptance.

While working with children as a substitute teacher when her own children were young, she witnessed bullying in the classroom. This inspired her to create Chili Chinchilla, a beautiful but different chinchilla. In today's world, it's more important than ever to teach children to accept those who appear to be different.

Donna has 3 grown children and 3 grandchildren. She resides in Plymouth, Massachusetts, where she is retired from a career in real estate, sales, and management.

Printed in the USA
CPSIA information can be obtained
at www.ICGtesting.com
LVHW072343261023
762232LV00016B/199